PUA'S PANIOLO PARADE

Written by Jolie Jean Cotton • Illustrated by Christine Joy Pratt

Dedications

For Mick, for Dawson, and in memory of a horse named Linger.
-Jolie Jean Cotton

For my cowgirl cousins, Laura and Louise.
-Christine Joy Pratt

Published and distributed by

ISLAND HERITAGE
P U B L I S H I N G

94-411 KŌʻAKI STREET, WAIPAHU, HAWAIʻI 96797
(800) 468-2800
hawaii4u@islandheritage.com
www.islandheritage.com

ISBN: 0-89610-428-1
First Edition   Second Printing - 2004

On Sunday, Paniolo Pua woke up early. The parade
was one week away, so she needed to get ready.

Pua started with the **one** most important thing...her gorgeous gray pony, Kiko. Paniolo Pua brushed Kiko and cleaned her hooves. Then they practiced riding.

On Monday, Paniolo Pua folded **two** fabulous flags, to be carried proudly in the parade. The first one was Hawaiian and the second one, American. Then Pua and Kiko practiced riding.

On Tuesday, Paniolo Pua gathered **three** pounds of pipi kaula. She placed the tasty treat into **four** sagging saddlebags, to share with the pāʻū team on parade day. Then Pua and Kiko practiced riding.

On Wednesday, Tūtū helped Pua finish weaving **five** fantastic lau hala hats for her paniolo pals, who would ride with a pāʻū princess. "A fine fit," Tūtū said, "and now it's time to practice your riding."

On Thursday, Paniolo Pua secured the last of **six** huge haku lei. There was one for each horse that would pull a parade wagon. Then Pua and Kiko practiced riding.

On Friday, Pua washed and ironed **seven** sassy palaka bandannas, one for each member of her family, so she could spot them in the crowd.

Then Paniolo Pua practiced riding with **eight** elegant ladies...the pāʻū princesses and the stunning pāʻū queen. There were **nine** high-stepping horses in all.

On Saturday, the crowd cheered as Paniolo Pua and Kiko rode with confidence through Makawao town.

Parade watchers filled the street, but Pua had no trouble finding her family.

After the parade, everyone gathered around a cozy campfire. Serenaded by **ten** super ʻukulele players, Paniolo Pua snuggled with Tūtū.
"You can be proud, my moʻopuna. Today, your riding was perfect," Tūtū said, kissing Pua's cheek.

"Kiko always comes through," Paniolo Pua said, and she nodded off to sleep.

GLOSSARY

Haku — *(ha-koo)* - A traditional lei making technique in which blossoms, leaves and fruits are braided or sewn face out into a background of greenery.

Moʻopuna — *(mo-oh-poo-nuh)* - Grandchild.

Lau hala — *(lau [rhymes with "cow"]-ha-luh)* - Pandanus leaf used in plaiting. Paniolo often adorn their lau hala hats with a lei of shells or fresh flowers.

Palaka — *(pa-la-kuh)* - Checked cloth used originally for work clothing. Paniolo used kerchiefs to protect the face against dust and sand.

Paniolo   *(pah-knee-o-low)* - Hawaiian cowboy.

Pā'ū   *(pah-oo)* - Skirt or sarong worn by female horseback riders.

Pipi kaula   *(pee-pee-cow-luh)* - Beef jerky. A convenient snack old time paniolo kept tucked in their pockets.